D0617137

FERNDALE PUBLIC LIBRARY

JE
H

Hoban, Julia.
    Amy loves the snow / by Julia Hoban ;
pictures by Lillian Hoban. -- New York :
Harper & Row, c1989.

    1 v. : ill. ; slj ps-1.

    SUMMARY: Amy builds a snowman with her
parents.
    ISBN 0-06-022395-2(lib. bdg.) : $9.89

51432

MAY 91

    1. Snow--Fiction. 2. Snowmen--Fiction. 3.
Parent and child--Fiction.   I. Title.

Ferndale Public Library
222 E. Nine Mile Rd
Ferndale, MI 48220

69

Amy Loves the Snow

by Julia Hoban

pictures by Lillian Hoban

3 9082 04226360 1

FERNDALE PUBLIC LIBRARY

Harper & Row, Publishers

For Frank

Amy Loves the Snow
Text copyright © 1989 by Julia Hoban
Illustrations copyright © 1989 by Lillian Hoban
Printed in Singapore. All rights reserved.

Library of Congress Cataloging-in-Publication Data
Hoban, Julia.
  Amy loves the snow.

  Summary: Amy builds a snowman with her parents.
  [1. Snow—Fiction. 2. Snowmen—Fiction. 3. Parent
and child—Fiction] I. Hoban, Lillian, ill. II. Title.
PZ7.H63487Ai 1989   [E]   87-45852
ISBN 0-06-022361-8
ISBN 0-06-022395-2 (lib. bdg.)

1 2 3 4 5 6 7 8 9 10
First Edition

Amy Loves the Snow

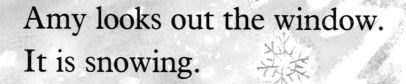

Amy looks out the window.
It is snowing.

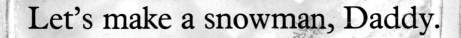

Let's make a snowman, Daddy.

Red mittens and red scarf for Amy.

Blue mittens and blue scarf for Daddy.

Amy's boots go *squeak squeak*.
Look, they leave small footprints.

Daddy's boots go *swish swish*.
Look, they leave big footprints.

Daddy and Amy make a big snowball.

That is the bottom of the snowman.

Amy makes a small snowball for the head.

The snow is so cold,
it goes through warm mittens.

Daddy, I caught a snowflake on my tongue.
It tastes cold and wet.

Here is Mommy.

She has a big orange carrot
for the snowman's nose.

Carrots taste better than snow.

Amy, give the snowman his nose.

Then we will go inside
and have some nice hot chocolate.